CHRISTMAS STORIES

for the Very Young

Selected and edited by Sally Grindley

Illustrated by Helen Cooper

KINGFISHER

NEW YORK

For Vanessa (S.G.)
For Jessica and Matthew (H.C.)

KINGFISHER
Larousse Kingfisher Chambers Inc.
95 Madison Avenue
New York, New York 10016

First American edition published in 1998
2 4 6 8 10 9 7 5 3
2TR/0399/SC/PW/EMA140

LIBRARY OF CONGRESS CATALOGING-IN-PUBLICATION DATA
Christmas stories for the very young / selected and edited by Sally
Grindley; illustrated by Helen Cooper.
p.   cm.
Contents: And there were shepherds—Imelda and the Dragon—Not
quite Christmas—Lucy's wish—Christmas lights—King Wod's
surprise present.
1. Christmas—Juvenile fiction. 2. Children's stories, English.
[1. Christmas—Fiction. 2. Short stories.]   I. Grindley, Sally.
II. Cooper, Helen (Helen F.), ill.
PZ5.C4755   1998
[E]—dc21   97-47594 CIP AC

ISBN 0-7534-5168-9
Printed in Hong Kong

CONTENTS

AND THERE WERE SHEPHERDS

Mary Rayner

And there were shepherds that night out on the hills looking after their sheep. The angel of the Lord appeared to them and told them that Jesus was born, and where they would find him. And there was light all about, and suddenly many, many angels, and more and more, all praising God and singing, "Glory be to God on high, Gloria, Gloria."

The sheep were huddled together in fright on the bare hillside. The great white light was fading now, and the voices gone. Below them the little group of shepherds was stamping out the embers of the fire.

The ewes watched. They couldn't believe what they saw. The shepherds were leaving, going off down the hill. They picked up the lamb with the hurt foot and carried him with them. The dog followed.

"Well!" said the first sheep.

5

"Going off without even seeing that we're all right. I don't think much of that!" said the second.

"Shepherds nowadays. Don't know their job. Off on some jaunt without so much as a word or a by your leave! No thought for others . . ." said the third.

"What about us? What if a wolf comes?" said the fourth, and they all looked over their shoulders into the dark, and huddled closer.

"Not up to it, that's what I say. Shouldn't ever have been hired," said the fifth. "It's all very well, all this *Gloria* nonsense, but who's going to look after us, that's what I'd like to know?"

"*And* they've taken my lamb," said the sixth. "And him with a bad foot."

"They could have left the dog at least," said the seventh. "But no, they've taken him as well."

"Typical," said the eighth. "People! You can't trust them an inch. One word from on high, and they're off on some fool's errand, responsibilities forgotten, all of us left to the wolves . . ."

She knelt on her front knees, and lurched down onto the ground. The others did the same, settling down around her, still grumbling. They waited in a tight little knot, every now and then eyeing the scatter of rocks where a wolf might be lurking.

The night was very dark, the stars brilliant. For the sheep it was a long wait until the first pale light showed above the hills in the east, and they could be easy. The day had dawned, and nothing had happened to them after all.

The sun rose higher, but no one came. The sheep wandered across the hillside, their bells tinkling, searching for grass among the dry rocks.

At last, about noon, they heard the barking of the dog, and behind him they saw the shepherds. The lamb could just be made out, following them.

The sheep trotted down the hill. The lamb bounded toward them, bleating in excitement.

"You'll never believe what I saw. All the way to Bethlehem we went, and into a stable, and there was a baby, and its mother, and her husband, and some cattle, and a donkey, and we all prayed—"

"Now just a minute, young fellow," said the ewe who was his mother. "Slow up."

"What d'you mean, prayed?" asked the first ewe. "Who to?"

"To God, of course," said the lamb simply. "It was a sign. The angels said so. The baby. A Savior, Christ the Lord."

"Well, I never," said the second ewe.

"Maybe that's why no wolves came last night," said the third ewe.

"I take it all back," said the fifth ewe.

"They were right to go after all," said the eighth, and they all nodded their heads, bleating. The bells clonked and tinkled across the hillside.

"And my foot's better," said the lamb, holding it up.

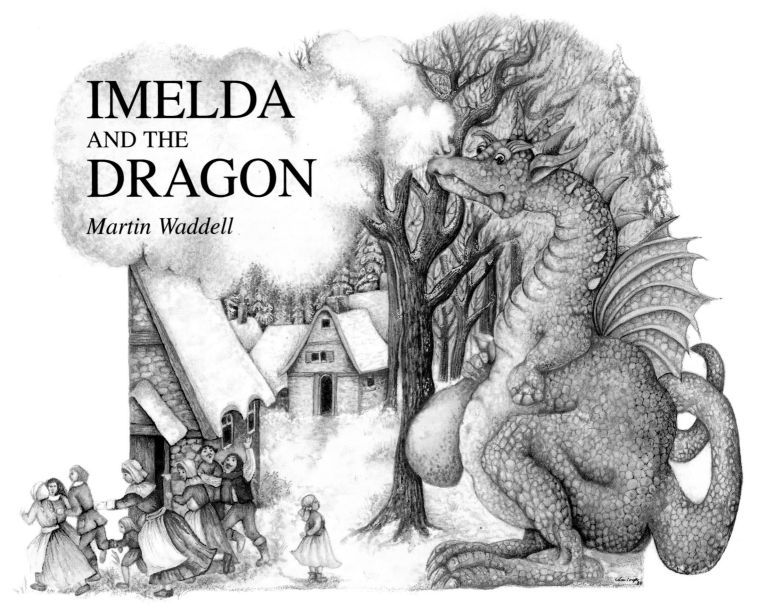

IMELDA
AND THE
DRAGON

Martin Waddell

Once there was a lonely Dragon.

It was lonely because it didn't meet many people, and when it did it toasted them, and then it ate them, which is what Dragons do to stop people stealing their Dragon gold.

One Christmas Day, the Dragon was out for a walk when it saw a village, so it thought it would toast the people and eat them. Puff-puff-puff! it went, warming up. The people saw the puffs, and they all ran away.

All except Imelda. Imelda thought that she *might* like the

Dragon. She didn't know for sure, because the Dragon only came around every ten years or so, and Imelda was only seven. She stayed where she was.

PUFF-PUFF-PUFF! Out of the snowy woods came the Dragon. It was big and green and scary, with a long tail and little fat wings. It came waddling up to Imelda, in a big cloud of smoke.

"Merry Christmas, Dragon!" said Imelda.

The Dragon heard someone squeak, from down there between its webby feet, but it wasn't able to see Imelda because of the smoke.

"Er . . . Merry Christmas," it said. Then it thought a bit. "What is Christmas?" it asked.

"It's when people are kind to each other, and give

each other presents," said Imelda. "It's *now*. This is Christmas Day."

"Nobody is ever kind to me," said the Dragon. "Nobody ever gives me presents. People just don't like Dragons."

Just then, Imelda's mom came running up to rescue Imelda from the Dragon. She was all dressed up in a suit of armor she had borrowed and she was waving a broadsword.

"Oh, goody! A fight!" said the Dragon, and it got ready to toast her.

"Stop!" cried Imelda. "I'm Imelda and that's my mom. I need my mom and I don't want her toasted."

"Toasting people is what Dragons do!" said the Dragon.

"Maybe that is *why* people don't like Dragons," said Imelda, who wasn't so sure about liking Dragons anymore herself.

"Do you think people would like me if I was kind?" asked the Dragon.

"Yes," said Imelda. "Try it."

"How do I begin?" asked the Dragon.

"Wish my mom a Merry Christmas," suggested Imelda.

"Er . . . Merry Christmas, Imelda's mom," said the Dragon.

"And a Merry Christmas to you, Dragon," said Imelda's mom, lowering her broadsword instead of whacking the Dragon with it, which wouldn't have done much good anyway, because the Dragon was too tough.

"Now give my mom a present," whispered Imelda.

And the Dragon gave Imelda's mom some of its gold.

"The Dragon is giving away gold!" all the villagers cried, and they came out of hiding and rushed into the village.

"Merry Christmas, Dragon!" they all cheered.

"Can I toast them?" said the Dragon.

"No," said Imelda. "Not at Christmas."

"Oh, all right!" said the Dragon, and it wished all the villagers a Merry Christmas and gave them gold, too.

"What a kind Dragon!" the villagers cried, and they started talking to the Dragon. They said how nice it was to meet a kind Dragon for a change, and they even gave it Christmas presents that they thought a Dragon might enjoy—like matches and kindling in case its fire went out, and blocks of ice for times when it got overheated. The village children climbed up on the Dragon and had Dragon rides, and they tickled it and made it laugh.

It was the best Christmas party the Dragon had ever been to. It was the first one, as well.

"I wish it could be Christmas every day!" the Dragon said, when the party was over and everybody was clearing up.

"Why?" said Imelda.

"So people would like me and be friends," said the Dragon.

Imelda thought for a bit.

"You could *pretend* it was Christmas Day every day," she told the Dragon. "Then you could be Christmas-kind to everyone instead of toasting them, and they would be Christmas-kind to you."

So that's what the Dragon did. It wasn't a nasty Dragon anymore, and it never toasted anybody or ate them ever again. All thanks to Imelda . . . and Christmas.

NOT *QUITE* CHRISTMAS

Dyan Sheldon

The streets were decked with tinsel and colored lights. The shops were decorated with angels and reindeer and laughing elves. Santa Claus was everywhere.

Belinda wanted to celebrate Christmas, too.

"Don't be silly," said Belinda's mother. "We don't celebrate Christmas. It's not our holiday."

But Belinda wanted to give presents. She wanted to make cookies shaped like stars. She wanted to sing carols. She wanted a Christmas tree. A Christmas tree covered with bright balls and winking lights. A tree with an angel right at its top. "But everybody celebrates Christmas," said Belinda.

"No they don't," said her mother. "Everyone has different holidays."

Belinda frowned. "Well, it *seems* like everyone celebrates Christmas."

"What about Uncle Frank?" asked Belinda's mother. "He doesn't celebrate Christmas. And my friend Sandra and her family? And your friend Emily across the street? And that nice doctor who took care of you when you were sick last summer? None of them celebrate Christmas either."

"Well everybody else does," said Belinda.

"Don't pay any attention," said Belinda's mother.

"It's hard not to," said Belinda.

Belinda's mother looked thoughtful.

"We could just have a tree," said Belinda. "It wouldn't have to be a big tree."

"There are plenty of trees outside," said Belinda's mother. "Where they belong."

Belinda went to school. The class was making paper chains. "Have you gotten your tree yet?" asked Amy.

Belinda wondered what she was going to do with her chain. "No," said Belinda, "not yet."

"I'm going to make my mother a special box to keep her pens in for Christmas," said David.

"I'm making my mother a vase," said Amy. "What are you making for your mother, Belinda?"

"I haven't decided," said Belinda.

"I'm asking Santa Claus to bring me a skateboard," said Amy. "What are you asking him to bring you?"

"I want a new bike," said David.

"What about you, Belinda?" asked Amy.

Belinda said, "I think my chain's too long."

Belinda and her mother and father were watching television. Three polar bears in Santa Claus hats were singing about Christmas.

"You're very quiet tonight, Belinda," said Belinda's father.

"Um," said Belinda.

"What's wrong?" asked her father.

"Nothing," said Belinda.

"What's that red and green thing in the wastepaper bin?" asked Belinda's mother.

"Nothing," said Belinda.

Belinda's mother lifted out Belinda's paper chain. "It doesn't look like nothing," she said.

"It's just something dumb we made at school."

Belinda's father said, "Oh."

Belinda's mother leaned over and whispered to him. "She's upset because we don't celebrate Christmas."

Belinda's father said, "Ah."

It was Christmas Eve. There was no one to play with. No one to watch a video with. Everybody was getting ready for Christmas. Except for Belinda. She sat looking out of the window at the falling snow.

"Are you going to sit there looking out of the window all day?" asked her mother. "Maybe," said Belinda.

"Why don't you go out and play?" asked her mother.

"I don't feel like it," said Belinda.

"I know. Why don't you take out your sled?"

"I don't feel like it," said Belinda.

"Why don't you watch a video then?"

"I don't feel like it," said Belinda.

"I know," said Belinda's mother. "Why don't you help me make some cookies?"

"Cookies?" said Belinda.

"Yes," said Belinda's mother. "I have some red and green sugar we could sprinkle on top."

"You mean like Christmas cookies?" asked Belinda. Belinda's mother smiled. "Not quite," she said.

Belinda's father came through the front door. "Something smells good," he called.

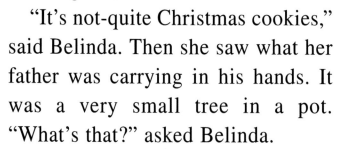

"It's not-quite Christmas cookies," said Belinda. Then she saw what her father was carrying in his hands. It was a very small tree in a pot. "What's that?" asked Belinda.

"It's a bay tree," said Belinda's father. "It was on sale in the supermarket." He put it on the table in front of the window. "I thought it would look pretty with your paper chain on it."

"Oh, and you know what?" said Belinda's mother. "I think I have some bows that would look nice on it as well."

"And how about hanging a cookie or two on it?" asked Belinda's father. "That would brighten it up."

Belinda looked at her mother. Then Belinda looked at her father. "You mean decorate it like a Christmas tree?" she asked.

"Well, not quite," said Belinda's father.

It was Christmas Day. Belinda's father was sitting in the living room, looking at the not-quite Christmas tree.

"You know," he said. "It looks very pretty. Especially with your chain. It's a shame there isn't anyone else to see it."

"You know," said Belinda's mother, "that's almost exactly what I was thinking. We have all those delicious cookies Belinda and I made and no one to help us eat them."

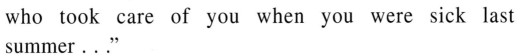

"I have an idea," said Belinda's father. "Why don't we invite some friends over to share them with us?"

"Because everybody's busy celebrating Christmas today," said Belinda glumly.

"Not everybody," said Belinda's mother. "There's Uncle Frank, and Sandra and her family, and Emily and her family, and that nice doctor who took care of you when you were sick last summer . . ."

Belinda was having a wonderful time. The living room was full of people. They were all eating cookies and drinking punch and playing games. The doctor who had taken care of Belinda when she was sick last summer was telling jokes. Everyone was laughing.

"And look what I found in the attic," said Belinda's mother hurrying into the room. "A string of lights from Belinda's birthday!"

"Perfect!" said Belinda's father. "We can put them on the tree."

Everyone stood in a circle to watch.

"Isn't it beautiful!" everyone cried when the lights went on.

"Oh, isn't this a lovely party," said Emily.

"It's the best party I've ever been to," said Sandra.

"Me too," said the doctor.

"Why, it's almost like a Christmas party," smiled Uncle Frank.

"Oh no, Uncle Frank," said Belinda. "Not quite."

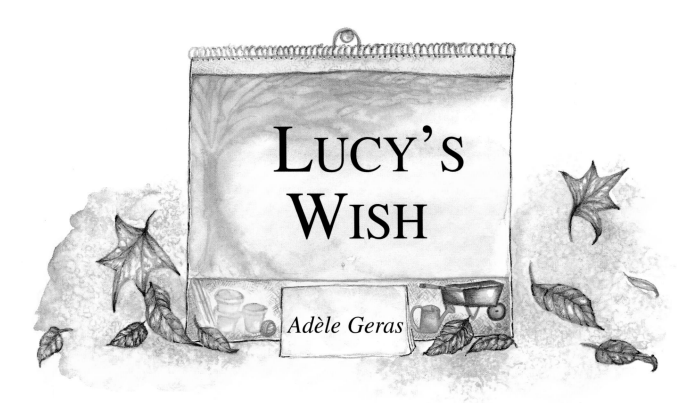

LUCY'S WISH

Adèle Geras

Every day Lucy watched the leaves falling from the trees in the garden and every day she asked her mother or sister or father what date it was, hoping that the answer would be Christmas Day.

One day, she asked her question in the supermarket as her mother was pushing her around in the trolley.

"It's only October the 23rd," said Lucy's mother, "but we're making the Christmas cake today."

Lucy smiled. She loved getting ready for Christmas.

At home, Lucy helped her mother prepare everything she needed to make the cake. Apart from the flour and eggs and sugar and margarine, there were all the packets they had bought in the supermarket: raisins, currants, sultanas, cherries, candied peel, and flaked almonds. Lucy put some of them into the bowl, and at the end she had to stir the squelchy beige mixture that was full of unexpected bits and lumps. As she stirred, she had to make a wish.

"What did you wish for?" Mom asked Lucy.

"That's a secret," said Lucy. "The wish doesn't work if you tell anyone what it is."

After the cake was made, days and days went by and nothing at all was said about Christmas. Outside in the garden, the trees were bare of leaves.

"What's the date?" asked Lucy.

"November the 30th," said her sister, Frances, who was eight. "I think we ought to start making the Christmas decorations."

"Yes, let's," said Lucy.

So Lucy and Frances sat in the kitchen with a big pot of paste and lots of colored paper, and made snakes of paper chains to go around the walls. All afternoon they sat at the big table by the window. The houses across the road grew darker and darker, until they looked like black paper cut-outs against the sky that turned pink as the sun went down, then mauve, then blue.

"Look," said Frances. "There's the first star. Make a wish, quickly."

Lucy closed her eyes and wished.

"What did you wish?" asked Frances.

"It's a secret," said Lucy. "The wish doesn't work if you tell anyone what it is."

After the decorations had been made, counting the days

to Christmas was easier. Lucy and Frances each had an Advent calendar, and every day they each opened a small door and looked at the picture inside. On December the 19th, Lucy's dad said:

"I've got the Christmas tree in the garage. Time to go and fetch all that stuff from the attic to put on it."

So Lucy and Frances and their dad went up into the attic to find the boxes full of what Lucy called the Tree Jewels. They brought the boxes downstairs and hung thin balls of shiny silver and purple and midnight blue from the

branches They looped golden tinsel around the tree, tied red ribbons into bows with long, trailing ends, and balanced small, silver paper-covered stars and moon shapes among the dark pine needles.

"Lucy," said Dad, "I'll hold you up while you put the Fairy Queen on top here. Don't forget to make a wish, now."

Lucy closed her eyes and wished. "What did you wish for?" asked Dad.

"It's a secret," said Lucy. "The wish doesn't work if you tell anyone what it is."

On Christmas Eve, Lucy couldn't sleep.

"Why can't you sleep?" asked Frances.

"I'm sad," said Lucy.

"How can you be sad on Christmas Eve?"

"I'm sad because my wish didn't come true. Even though I wished for it three times."

"What did you wish for?" asked Frances.

"It was silly. I don't want to say." Lucy turned her face into the pillow.

"Well, go to sleep now," said Frances. "It's Christmas Day tomorrow. You'll be happy then."

Lucy thought about her wish. Perhaps it really had been

silly to hope that the garden, which was full of fallen leaves and bare trees and dark earth, could be made pretty again. Lucy knew that leaves and flowers came in the spring, but it seemed unfair to her that when everything *inside* was so bright and beautiful the garden should be so gray and empty.

"Maybe," she thought, "I'll try again. Just once more." Lucy closed her eyes and wished. Then she fell asleep.

In the morning, Frances woke up first.

"Lucy," she whispered. "Wake up. Let's see what's in our stockings." Lucy woke up and together the two girls ate the tangerines and nuts and raisins that someone had put into their Christmas stocking during the night.

"It's very sunny," said France. "You can tell even though the curtains are closed. It's so light."

"Let's open them," said Lucy. "You pull that one and I'll pull this one."

The curtains opened.

"Look!" whispered Lucy. "Oh, Frances, look! My wish came true in the night."

The garden glittered in the sun. Every branch and twig and blade of grass, every roof and windowsill, the dark brown earth and the green tops of the hedges: everything was thick with snow. The window of Lucy and Frances's bedroom had frost all around the edges of the glass, like a border of white flowers.

"It's lovely!" said Lucy. "I never thought it would look as pretty as that."

"Is that what you wished for?" asked Frances. "Did you wish for snow?"

"I didn't know I wished for it," said Lucy, "but I suppose I must have."

"What did you say, then?"

"I just closed my eyes and said: I wish the garden could be decorated for Christmas."

"Well," said Frances, "it is decorated. Let's go and tell Mom and Dad."

They ran into their Mom and Dad's room.

"Wake up!" said Lucy. "It's Christmas Day, and my wish came true!"

CHRISTMAS LIGHTS

Angela Bull

Christmas was coming. Amy sang "Away in a Manger" at school, and smelled mince pies cooking when she got home.

A neighbor, Mrs. Robinson, popped her head around the kitchen door. "I'm taking a load of kids into town tonight to see the Christmas lights," she said. "Would Amy like to come?"

"Yes, please," said Amy's mom.

Mrs. Robinson collected quite a crowd; enough to fill two cars. They all lived near Amy: Zoë and her best friend Donna; Peter with the glasses, and Ian with the leather jacket; and Jenny who had long fair hair. Amy was much the smallest. There were grown-ups as well—and there was a dog. He was a dachshund called Chips. Amy liked him at once.

It was squished in the car. People talked and laughed above Amy's head. Chips sat on the floor. Amy could feel his smooth coat beside her knees.

The cars stopped in a big parking lot.

"Come back here if you get lost," said Mrs. Robinson to everyone. Then they scrambled out—all except Chips.

"He'd better stay here. He might get stepped on," said Mrs. Robinson. She shut the car door. Chips peeped sadly through the window.

Amy forgot about him, for the first Christmas lights swung high in the air above the entrance to the parking lot. All along the street they went, like a glittering necklace of red and silver beads, around a curve and out of sight.

"Come on. This is only the beginning," said Mrs. Robinson. The children hurried ahead. Their voices floated back. "Wow!" "Excellent!"

The grown-ups chatted together. Amy came last, following.

At a corner, where two necklaces met, a Santa Claus

was outlined in lights against the black sky. His coat was red; his beard was white. One hand was pointing.

"He's showing us the way to go," said Mrs. Robinson.

Santa after Santa hung above the street, all pointing. There were colored lights in the shops they passed, and silver trees, and strings of shimmering tinsel. Amy couldn't help stopping to look at everything; and she stopped, too, by a cart selling hot chestnuts, which smelled delicious. But she was getting left behind. She ran along the crowded pavement, until she could see Ian's leather jacket again, and Jenny's long fair hair.

Suddenly, above them, was a Santa Claus without a beard. His white lights had gone out.

"Here we are," said Mrs. Robinson. "This is the square."

Everywhere, shining lights swooped and zigzagged. Strands gathered like maypole ribbons, and swung away to distant corners. Among them flew angels on bright wings of light. Trumpeters blew silver trumpets, and drummer boys beat drums of scarlet and gold.

The tree stood in the middle. Amy had never seen such a tall one. It reached up and up, as if it was stretching to touch the flying angels and the little drummer boys. More lights spangled its branches; white ones, silver ones. Crowning it was a five-pointed golden star. Christmas carol music floated out of loudspeakers. Some people were singing along with it. Amy threaded her way through them toward the tree. The blaze of its lights dazzled her. She gazed, blinked—and then stared around.

Where was Mrs. Robinson? Where was Jenny's long hair, and Ian's leather jacket? She could only see the dark shapes of strangers, crowds of them, filling the square.

Amy's heart began to thump. Though she was surrounded by more people than she'd ever seen before, she felt horribly alone. Alone and abandoned. Lost.

"Go back to the car if you're lost," Mrs. Robinson had said. But where was the car? Amy looked all around, shaking with fright.

Five roads branched off the square. Which one led to the parking lot? Santa Clauses shone at every corner, and suddenly Amy remembered. The Santa she wanted had no lights in his beard.

She saw him almost at once, pointing across at her. Feeling much happier, she ran up to him, and turned down his street, under the necklace of red and silver beads. She only had to go the way the Santas *weren't* pointing. Here was the chestnut seller, packing up his cart. Here were the shops with silver trees and tinsel. She was going to be all right. She came to the last Santa Claus. She reached the parking lot.

"Woof!" Before she had time to look for the car, she heard Chips barking. He was standing on his hind legs on the back seat. Mrs. Robinson had left the window open a crack, and his little nose was poking through the gap.

"Hello!" said Amy. She put her fingers to the crack, and Chips licked them. Then she smelled hot chestnuts. The chestnut seller, wheeling his cart past, stopped.

"Now, love, are you lost?" he asked.

"No," said Amy. "Just waiting."

"Here," he said. "My last bag." He dropped a paper bag of hot chestnuts into Amy's cold hands.

Amy opened the bag, peeled a chestnut, broke it in two, ate half herself, and gave Chips half through the open window. She heard his tail thump the car seat as it wagged.

And that was the nicest moment in the whole evening.

"Amy!" It was Mrs. Robinson. "Thank goodness you're here! I was so worried. I had no idea there'd be such a crowd; and I didn't know where you'd gone to."

"You said come back to the car if we were lost," Amy explained.

"You were quite right. Good girl! Thank you for being so sensible." Everyone else gathered around. Jenny smiled at Amy through her veil of long hair. The boys grinned.

Amy sat on the back seat of the car, with Chips on her knee, sharing out her chestnuts. Above them all the necklaces of lights swooped and glittered; but it was time to go home.

KING WOD'S SURPRISE PRESENT

Chris Powling

King Wod was very, very rich.

He had so much money he could have filled up the stocking of every kid in the land—yes, including yours if you'd been around—and still had plenty left over. So why was it he *hated* Christmas?

The reason was this. More than anything else in the world, King Wod wanted a surprise present on Christmas morning.

Is that all?

Aha . . . let's not forget how rich he was. Year after year it was the same. Whatever present he was given—it didn't matter how wonderful—King Wod had one already. For instance:

A horse with multicolored hooves for riding on rainbows;

A book of answers to every question a teacher can ask;

A picnic basket that glowed in the dark when you took it on a midnight feast;

A pillow for singing you to sleep;

A special puddle for splashing indoors without wetting the carpet . . .

But why go on? "I've got one of those," King Wod always said.

Eventually, early one Christmas morning before the sun was even up, he lost his temper. He kicked over his royal throne, tore his royal cloak in half and sent his royal crown spinning straight through the palace window.

"Can't anyone bring me a surprise present?" he roared.

"Send for the royal wizard!"

"I'm already here, your Majesty."

"Well, don't just stand there, Wizard. *Do* something. That's an order!"

ABRA – CA – ZAM!

"Eh?"

Quick as a blink, there was King Wod in a dark, snow-covered forest. "Where am I?" he asked. "The North Pole? Just wait till I get back to the palace—that wizard is in deep, deep trouble."

Right now, though, it was King Wod himself in deep, deep trouble. The snow was knee-high in some places and up to his armpits in other places, and it was hard to tell one place from the other. Soon he was as stiff and chilly as an icicle. "And if I don't keep moving that's what I will be," he groaned. "A king-sized icicle. Wait, is that a house I see over there?"

With a sigh of relief he trudged toward a tiny, snow-thatched cottage on the forest's edge.

The cottage was empty.

Lived in, yes. There was a fire ready in the grate, food ready in the pantry, and comfy furniture ready in the sitting room. "Where's the owner, though?" asked the King. "And why are there no paper chains and Christmas cards and a tree in the corner with Christmas lights?"

For there was no sign of Christmas in the cottage at all.

Except, that is, for an Advent calendar on the mantelpiece. It was open at December the 24th. "Christmas Eve," King Wod said. Somehow this made the small, snow-bound cottage seem emptier than ever.

No wonder the King felt lonely. Was this to be his first-ever Christmas on his own? "Better get warm for a start," he told himself. "Then keep busy. That's what I must do."

He was quite right, of course. It was fun to chop down a tree in the forest and stand it in a corner of the sitting

room—especially when he found a big box of Christmas decorations tucked away in a cupboard under the stairs. Putting these up was fun, too. So was lighting the fire and laying the table for Christmas dinner.

After this King Wod drew a fancy Christmas card for the cottage owner. He stood it on the mantelpiece. Then, just in case, he made a fancy gift box as well. Inside, he put a note saying:

> *"This space is reserved for a present from King Wod. It can be a book of answers to every question a teacher can ask, a picnic basket that glows in the dark for midnight feasts, a horse for riding on rainbows . . . anything you like. You choose."*

And he put the gift box under the Christmas tree.

Last of all, for the best fun of all, he set out an extra place at the table. "Well," he sighed. "You never know . . ."

And he fell sound asleep in front of the fire.

It was daylight that woke him up. That and the sound of sleigh bells. The door swung open and in came just the sort of plump, comfy-looking old man you'd expect to live in a cottage like this. Mind you, with frost in his eyebrows, ice in his beard, and snowflakes melting on his red suit and empty sack, it took Wod at least two seconds to recognize him.

"Santa Claus!" he gasped.

"Hello," said Santa Claus. "Who are you?"

"Er . . . King Wod, actually. I'm sorry about—"

"King Wod?"

Santa stared at him in astonishment. "You mean that letter from the wizard was *real*? About how you were bringing me . . . bringing me . . ."

His voice trailed away as his eye fell on the decorations and the dinner table, the card on the mantelpiece and the present under the tree.

"Oh, my goodness gracious!" he gasped. "How did you know?"

"Know?" said Wod. "Know what?"

"That I haven't had a real Christmas *ever*."

"Haven't you?"

"Before it comes, I'm always too busy. After it goes, I'm always too tired. And now you've organized everything for me. Bless you, your Majesty! I'm so grateful. However did you think of such a lovely surprise present?"

"Surprise present?"

"My very own Christmas," said Santa Claus. "It's the first I've ever had."

"It's the first I've ever given," said King Wod, thoughtfully.

But already he knew it wouldn't be the last.

Wod never forgot the lesson his clever wizard had taught him. After all, if you're a king who has everything, *receiving* a surprise present is bound to be difficult. But *giving* one is easy.

Later, after he'd made the wizard Prime Minister, King Wod said: "There is just one problem, though. What should I put in the box I left under the fir tree? Santa couldn't decide which present he like best."

"Simple," smiled the wizard.

And he whispered in King Wod's ear.

I'd love to tell you what he suggested. But that would spoil the surprise.